Tree Fu Team!

We need to turn the magic on,
We need to save the day, come on!

SCAN THIS CODE ON YOUR SMART PHONE
TO DOWNLOAD TREE FU FUN ACTIVITY SHEETS!

Alternatively, visit www.**treefutombooks**.co.uk

BANTAM
BOOKS

TREE FU TOM: Tree Fu Team!
A BANTAM BOOK 978 0 857 51162 1

First published in Great Britain by Bantam, an imprint of Random House Children's Publishers UK
A Random House Group Company.

This edition published 2014

1 3 5 7 9 10 8 6 4 2

Tree Fu Tom created by Daniel Bays.
Based on the episode 'One for All!', written by Sindy McKay.
TREE FU TOM word and device marks are trade marks of the British Broadcasting Corporation
and FremantleMedia Limited and are used under licence.
TREE FU TOM device marks © BBC and FremantleMedia Limited MMX.
The "BBC" word mark and logo are trade marks of the British Broadcasting Corporation
and are used under licence. BBC Logo © BBC 1996. The "CBeebies" word mark and logo are
trade marks of the BBC and are used under licence. CBeebies Logo © BBC 2001.
Licensed by FremantleMedia Limited.

www.TreeFuGo.com

Set in Trebuchet MS Regular.

Bantam Books are published by Random House Children's Publishers UK,
61-63 Uxbridge Road, London W5 5SA

www.randomhousechildrens.co.uk

Addresses for companies within The Random House Group Limited can be found at:
www.randomhouse.co.uk/offices.htm

THE RANDOM HOUSE GROUP Limited Reg. No. 954009

A CIP catalogue record for this book is available from the British Library.

Printed in China

The Random House Group Limited supports the Forest Stewardship Council® (FSC®), the leading
international forest-certification organization. Our books carrying the FSC label are printed
on FSC®-certified paper. FSC is the only forest certification scheme supported by the leading
environmental organizations, including Greenpeace. Our paper procurement policy can be found
at www.randomhouse.co.uk/environment

Tree Fu Team!

One day in Treetopolis, Tom, Ariela, Twigs and Squirmtum were warming up for Squizzle practice. Rickety was training them. They had a big Squizzle tournament coming up soon but they hadn't been playing very well.

"Right, everyone," said Rickety, "Training will be a little different today. You must learn that playing Squizzle isn't **just** about hitting the wingseeds. It's about playing together as a team."

"OK!" cried Twigs. "Wait . . . I don't get it."

"Tom, it's time we put your skills as a leader to use on the Squizzle pitch," announced Rickety. "You are team captain!"

TIME TO PLAY!

"OK, let's go team!" shouted
Tom. "Twigs, go left!"
Tom threw the Squizzle left,
but Twigs wasn't listening, so
he wasn't there to catch it.
Ariela picked up the Squizzle and whistled
loudly at Squirmtum. PHWEE! But Squirmtum didn't
realize, and the Squizzle nearly hit him on the
head. Luckily, Tom caught it just in time!

Rickety shook his head and called everyone over. "To be a great team you need to **listen** and **talk** to each other, **focus** and have a **good leader**." Rickety sighed as he looked at each member of the team – everyone looked very confused. "Or you could just use the **Enchanted Squizzle** when you play . . ." he suggested mysteriously. The whole team buzzed with excitement.

Rickety picked up an old, dusty book. As he opened it, dust flew everywhere. "The legend says that the team who wins the Enchanted Squizzle from the **Squizzle Master** will be able to play perfectly and be unbeatable," explained Rickety. "Wowzers!" said Twigs.

"The Squizzle who?" asked Tom.

"The Squizzle **Master** is a legend. He is the best Squizzle player in Treetopolis and he guards the Enchanted Squizzle," replied Rickety.

"How do we find it, Rickety?" asked Tom.

"I don't know where it is . . ." Rickety said. Everyone sighed in disappointment. "But, I once heard a clue about it: **'To find it, seek a purple weed. Shout out loud! Defeat the seed.'"**

"I've seen a purple weed!" shouted Tom, as he eagerly flew straight up into the air ready to race off and find it.

"Have we forgotten something, Team Captain?" asked Rickety.

"Oh, yes! We can find it together as a team!" cried Tom. Everyone cheered.

"It's all for one and one for all!" said Twigs.

"To find the Enchanted Squizzle, we're going to need Big World Magic. So, we need to do the moves that turn our magic powers on."

IT'S TIME FOR TREE FU!

Slide to the side, and jump right back!
Hold your hands up high . . .
Touch your nose.
Now make a pose!
Touch your knees,
and run with me!

"Look!" said Tom.
"The sapstone
in my belt is
glowing. Moving
turned our
magic on!"

The team followed Tom and found the purple weed.

"Hmm," thought Tom, "the clue said: '**Shout out loud, defeat the seed**'." Twigs didn't need telling twice! He flew straight up to the weed and started shouting.

"Careful, Twigs," warned Tom. "It might be dangerous!" But it was too late – the weed started firing seeds at Twigs! Tom quickly did a *Go Shield* spell.

Tom looked at his friends. "Right, we can **all** do this, but we need to work as a team," he said. Everyone listened to Tom's plan.

Twigs flew up to the weed to draw its fire, and Squirmtum threw his helmet to Ariela, who used it to hit a flying seed straight back into the weed. Working as a team, they defeated the weed!

"Yes, we did it!" shouted Twigs.

The purple weed fell to the ground. Its leaves
unfolded to reveal . . .

"A clue!" cried Tom. He read it out loud: "'**Seek
to find the cavern wall. But listen well or you
may fall!**'"

Squirmtum's face lit up. "Don't worry, I know
the caverns like the back of my hands!"
he said proudly.

The team made
their way down
into the dark cave.

The only light was from Flicker, who was inside
Squirmtum's helmet.

Suddenly, there was a loud THUD as Tom and Ariela
tripped over.

"Watch out, Twigs!" warned Ariela.

But Twigs wasn't listening, so he tripped over,
too! "You could have warned me!" he cried.

Suddenly, Ariela spotted something floating above them close to the cavern wall.

"I've found the next clue!" she cried as she flew up to get the scroll. "'**Squizzle ahead! Keep going straight. Focus and soon your game will be great!**'"

"Last one there's a rotten mushroom!" shouted Twigs as he zoomed off, quickly followed by Ariela and Squirmtum.

"Wait!" Tom called after them. "We need to stick together!"

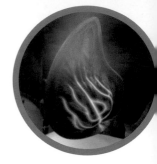

The team found themselves in a large cave. The Enchanted Squizzle was lit up by a beam of light.

Twigs started to dance around. "We've found it! Come on . . ."

Tom stopped him. "Hold on, Twigs. We need to be careful!"

Ariela noticed some footprints carved into the stone floor. "I reckon we're supposed to follow those," she said.

"Step back and let the cavern expert lead the way!" announced Squirmtum.

As they walked, Tom reminded everyone what the clue had said: **'Focus and soon your game will be great.'**

Squirmtum began telling everyone a story about a time he had been really focused, when suddenly, the cave began to shake.

"**Treequake!**" shouted the Treelings. Squirmtum had been so distracted telling his story that he had wandered off the path. The others flew safely up into the air, but Squirmtum couldn't fly!

Squirmtum was stranded.

"Help!" he cried.

"Get me off here!"

"It's too dangerous for us to try to carry Squirmtum. We'll have to use Big World Magic to move those columns so he can use them as steps," decided Tom.

It was time to use the MEGA MOVER spell.

TREE FU GO!

"Imagine you are picking up a tiny leaf. Reach across your body, pick up, move to the other side and release.

Now imagine you are picking up a heavy box. Grab, lift, move to the other side and release.

Now, clap and say 'Mega Mover!' to send the magic to me!"

Tom moved all the columns so they were in a line. "OK, Squirmtum. You need to jump on to the column in front of you!" shouted Tom.

"OK, Tom," called Squirmtum, nervously. As he stood up, the column wobbled, but he bravely jumped on to the column in front of him.

"Great work, Squirmtum! Just two more jumps!" called Tom. It took a lot of focus, but Squirmtum made it safely across the columns. Everyone cheered!

"Come on, team. We can't let a little treequake set us back! Let's go!" said Tom as he led them towards the back of the cave.

The team stopped and excitedly looked around. A loud voice boomed around the cave. "I am the great and powerful Squizzle Master. You have made it to the final round in your quest for the Enchanted Squizzle."

"Tell me what you have learned today and the Enchanted Squizzle will be yours!" the voice continued.

"What do you mean?" Tom asked, confused.

"I need to see that you can work together as a team. You must hit and spin every wingseed and every one of you must play a part," the voice explained.

Tom called his team into a huddle. "We can do this! We just need to remember what Rickety said about being a great team!"

"GO-O-O TEAM!" they all shouted.

As they played with the Enchanted Squizzle:

Tom **led the team** by giving them a game plan.

Twigs **listened** to Tom's plan.

Ariela **talked** to her teammates.

And Squirmtum **focused** on the game.

The team hit and spun all the wingseeds!

"Not bad! But there are two things you should know," said the Squizzle Master. "One, the Squizzle Master is really . . ."
The team saw a very familiar shape moving out from the shadows.
"Me!" said Rickety.
Just then, the cave began to rumble and shake . . .

The team had damaged the ceiling during their Squizzle game! Rocks began to fall down, trapping Rickety inside a hollow of the cave.

"We're **doomed!**" wailed Twigs.

"No, we're not," said Tom, "We just need to work as a team to smash the rocks before they fall on us. But first, we'll have to use Big World Magic to freeze the rocks in mid-air."

It was time to do the SUPER FREEZE spell.

TREE FU GO!

"This is a really fast spell; look out for the freezes.

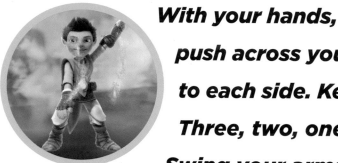

With your hands, push across your body to each side. Keep going fast! Three, two, one, FREEZE. Swing your arms forward like you're swimming. Keep going fast! Three, two, one, FREEZE. Now clap, say 'Super Freeze!' to send the magic to me."

The spell froze the rocks in mid-air.

"Right team, let's break these up using the Enchanted Squizzle!" cried Tom.

Everyone took turns throwing the Enchanted
Squizzle at the rocks until they had broken all of
them into smaller pieces.

Ariela took the final shot and broke the rock
that had trapped Rickety. As he walked free,
the Enchanted Squizzle fell to the ground . . .
in two pieces.

"Oh no, it's broken," wailed Twigs.

"Ah, that's the second thing I wanted to tell
you . . ." started Rickety.

"There's no such thing as an Enchanted Squizzle.
You've been playing with the same Squizzle you
did before!" continued Rickety.

"What do you mean?" asked Tom.

Rickety smiled, "You played well because you
learned the skills to play as a team. Teamwork is
your special power!"

"Aw, teamwork doesn't have any power!"
laughed Twigs.

Tom thought for a moment. "Maybe it does,
Twigs! It helped us defeat the purple weed."

"And rescue Rickety!" said Ariela

"It even helped us smash the rocks,"
added Squirmtum.

"That's what I said, teamwork has power!"
Twigs said. Everyone giggled.

Later, back at the Squizzle pitch, the team were finishing their practice.

"So that's why you sent us on that crazy journey, Rickety – to learn about teamwork," realized Ariela.

"I did say that training would be different today!" laughed Rickety.

"Thanks for being the best coach a team could ever have, Rickety. We're bound to win the tournament now!" said Tom. "TREE FU TEAM!"